THE
EXPERT EXPE...

A Classroom Companion to *The Expert Effect*

Zach Rondot

Grayson McKinney

Suria Ali-Ahmed

COPYRIGHT

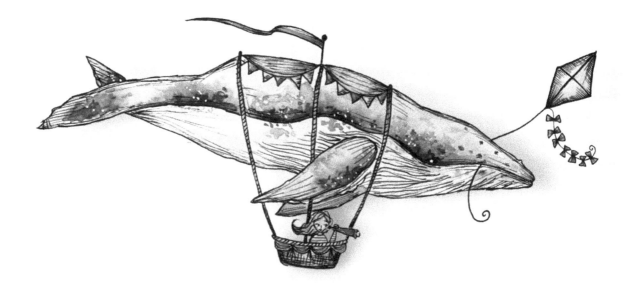

DEDICATION

For all of my students—past, present, and future—
may you dream big, push your comfort zone,
and pursue your passions.
-Z.R.

To Locke, Dempsey, and Madigan—
never stop exploring!
-G.McK.

To my husband, children, and mom—thank you for your
everlasting support. To my students—the journey is the
dream, inspire others, and always be kind.
-S.A.

Welcome, dear learners. We know why you're here. You're chasing adventure like a brave buccaneer!

Sailing the high seas and surfing the web, Searching for answers from Algiers to Zagreb.

No, nothing can stop you! You're a kid on a mission, and it's finally time for your big expedition.

You're not after riches
like silver or gold...
The thing that you seek
can't be bought
or be sold.

Yes, you're after
knowledge—
there's so much to know.
It's worth more than
treasure in a
ship's cargo hold!

So off you must go
with your sails
flown unfurled.
To get the whole story,
go out into the world!

But we have to inform you
of a little-known truth...
Some solutions are hidden
like the Fountain of Youth.

No one we know has all of the answers—
Not professors or pilots or doctors or dancers!

But please, oh please, don't let
that stop you from going!
There're so many skills
that you ought to be growing.

The whole planet is bursting
with people of knowledge
Who you can encounter
before you reach college.

Learn right from these experts
through FaceTime or Zoom.
That's sure to help break down
the walls of your room!

We're here to extract you
from your old comfort zone,
And the good news is
no one must go it alone.

Generate questions and sort them just so,
Then ask a true EXPERT what you want to know.

Experienced, exciting, purposeful, real...
They'll teach and empower—that's a really big deal!

But the experts you'll learn from didn't know overnight...
It was patience and practice that helped them take flight.

They all made some blunders (as you likely will too)
But growing from errors is the number one rule.

For learning can come with some challenging parts.
It's not all smooth sailing—it stops and then starts!

If you make a mistake, don't worry, don't sweat.
It just means you haven't quite mastered it YET!

Now, where will you study?
A museum or zoo?
Learning on field trips
assures you it's true.

And whether you travel
by web, bus, or car,
Asking an expert
can help you go far.

So please don't just sit there
with thoughts in your head.
You have to apply your
new knowledge instead!

What amazing new app
or device will you make...
Or community service
project undertake?

You could start your own podcast—let your voice be heard loud.
Or become a YouTuber—you'd feel really proud!

Create a new website with clickable links—
That would help guide your audience
to think up new thinks!

And now that you've started, you can't hold it hidden.
Keeping it all to yourself is forbidden!
The last part of our formula's crucially key...
You have to make something for the whole world to see!

You've asked,
"Who can we learn from?"
Now, who will **YOU** teach?
Who will be present for your
big keynote speech?

You see, learning's a cycle that goes on without end,
And part of that process means teaching a friend.

When you share what you've learned, it cements things in place.
It grows and expands on your own knowledge base.

Teach to your grandparents or some little tyke...
When **YOU** are the expert, **YOU** hold the mic!

From expos to plays, there're so many choices.
Use the tech in your hands to amplify voices!

ARCHEOLOGY   CHEMISTRY   AVIATION

While you may not be privy to your teachers' inten
It's the concept of "schooling" **YOU** can help reinv

May *The Expert Effect*
be their guide to take chances
And watch all astonished
as kids' learning advances.

School should be joyful—a fun place to be—
Where passions are fed like you'd water a tree.

A place where
all students
can grow
root to twig...

A place where
you'll never forget to
DREAM BIG!

AUTHORS' MESSAGE

Dear Learners,

There once was a time when the classroom teacher had to be the expert in everything they taught, but times have changed. We like to think of the modern teacher as an information agent—making connections between you and all the right people at the right time to inspire you to learn and become anything you want. That could mean taking you on field trips in real life, video chatting with experts in the field, or collaborating with other classrooms around the world. We've got the technology to connect people anywhere at any time so we might as well use it!

We hope you use your learning to improve your life, improve the lives of others, and improve the world around you. After all, knowledge is power, and we want you to use your power for good. To get started, ask yourself these three questions:

Who will you learn from?

Your favorite author? A sports star? A real-life scientist?

What will you create?

A podcast? A useful app? A work of art?

Who will you teach?

Your classmates? Your family? Your city council?

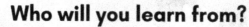

The possibilities are endless, so dream big!

Mr. Rondot & Mr. McKinney

A NOTE TO EDUCATORS

First of all, thank you. Thank you for being a teacher and going above and beyond to create memorable learning experiences for your students. We know first hand that this work is not always easy, but we've also seen the many benefits of prioritizing deep learning in classrooms around the world.

Our goal in creating this book was to give you an intriguing and powerful guide to use with your students year after year when introducing, revisiting, or launching any type of authentic research projects in your classroom. We also wrote a book specifically for you called *The Expert Effect: A Three-Part System to Break Down the Walls of Your Classroom and Connect Your Students to the World* in which we thoroughly explain how to apply these deep learning concepts.

We've created a website to help you even further: ExpertEffectEDU.com. There, you'll find free resources to help guide you on your own "expert" expeditions. We'd love for you to join the conversation by sharing your experience and your students' learning by adding to our hashtag, #ExpertEffectEDU, on social media.

Have fun connecting your students to the world!

Zach & Grayson

ILLUSTRATOR'S STATEMENT

Art is a part of me—a gift that I cherish. With the practice of swirls and twists of crayons, paints, and pencils, an inner creativity was unleashed at a young age. My art transformed and grew as I grew. My mother, my first art teacher, was a constant guide throughout my journey. I was inspired by different artists—Lewis Carroll's illustrations in *Alice's Adventures in Wonderland*, Cathie Shuttleworth's illustrations in *The Children's Treasure of Classic Poetry*, and even Tim Burton's drawings of his imaginative characters. My art took on its own style, which is what you see today in the illustrations in *The Expert Expedition*. For this book, I used watercolor and gouache paints, Prisma colored pencils, and ink pens on mixed medium paper to create the pictures.

Suria Ali-Ahmed is a high school English teacher who has a passion for art. She lives in Michigan with her husband and children.

Suria Ali-Ahmed

MEET THE EXPERTS

Grayson is first and foremost a teacher, but he could really get used to calling himself a writer. He mostly co-authored his first book for grownups, *The Expert Effect*, in a chair next to a fireplace at his local Starbucks, but wrote this, his first book for kids, from his house in Michigan, where he lives with his family. You can find his wife, three children, and their dog pictured in this book!

Grayson McKinney

Zach is a 4th-grade teacher in Michigan. He has taught elementary school since 2013. When he started his journey as a teacher, he never would have imagined he would be a published author. Writing and sharing messages with teachers and students has become a true passion and he hopes you're ready to take your learning to the next level as you set off on your *Expert Expedition*.

Zach Rondot

Printed in the USA
CPSIA information can be obtained
at www.ICGtesting.com
JSHW071917010224
56309JS00009B/26